BBC CHILDREN'S BOOKS
Published by the Penguin Group
Penguin Books Ltd, 80 Strand, London WC2R 0RL, England
Penguin Group (Australia), 250 Camberwell Road, Camberwell, Victoria 3124,
Australia (a division of Pearson Australia Group Pty Ltd)
First published by BBC Worldwide Ltd, 2002
Text and design © BBC Children's Character Books, 2002
This edition published by BBC Children's Books, 2006
CBeebies & logo™ BBC. © BBC 2002
BBC & logo © and ™ BBC 1996
10 9 8 7 6 5 4 3 2 1
Written by Iona Treahy
Based on a script by Jimmy Hibbert
Based upon the television series
Bob the Builder © 2006 HIT Entertainment Ltd. and Keith Chapman.
The Bob the Builder name and character and the Wendy, Spud, Roley,
Muck, Pilchard, Dizzy, Lofty and Scoop characters are trademarks of
HIT Entertainment Ltd. Registered in the UK.
With thanks to HOT Animation
www.bobthebuilder.com
ISBN 1 40590182 9
Printed in Italy

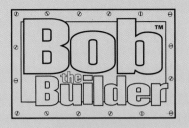

Pilchard Steals
the Show

CHILDREN'S BOOKS

Bob and the machines were building a barn
for Farmer Pickles's sheep.

"Can we fix it?" Scoop called to everyone

"Yes, we can!" the other machines replied.

Roley made the ground nice and smooth, ready for the barn to stand on.

As they were working, Bob heard a whistling sound. The sound came again, and Bob spotted Farmer Pickles on the other side of the hedge.

Farmer Pickles was training Scruffty to sit, walk and roll over.

"That's really good. Well done, you two!" called Bob.

"I have high hopes for Scruffty winning the dog show today," said Farmer Pickles.

"Hey, Bob!" said Scoop. "How about entering Pilchard in the show? She's just as smart as Scruffty – I bet she could win."

"I'm sorry Scoop, but it's a dog show – no cats allowed," chuckled Farmer Pickles.

"Oh well, never mind Scoop," said Bob.

Scoop, however, was determined to enter the show with Pilchard. He went back to the yard to look for her.

"Pilchard!" he called. "Pil-chaaard, come!"

Pilchard came out, wondering what all the noise was about.

"There, see?" said Scoop. "You came when I called you. It is going to be easy-peasy to train you. What do you think, Pilchard?"

"Miaow!" cried Pilchard.

Scoop tried whistling at Pilchard, but the noise only frightened her. But he wasn't giving up on his plan to enter the show. Eventually, he persuaded Pilchard to sit in his scoop, and off they went to the dog show.

When they got to the enclosure,
Pilchard spotted a mouse and shot
straight past Scoop, after it.

"Pilchard! Come back!" cried Scoop. "We don't have much time before the show starts."

Pilchard turned and walked towards Scoop, leaving the mouse to escape.

"Good Pilchard!" said Scoop. But as he moved forward he got tangled in the flags around the enclosure.

"Oh no!" squealed Scoop. "Help, Pilchard! I'm stuck!"

Pilchard ran to Farmer Pickles's farm to get some help.

Bob and the team were just finishing putting the roof on the new barn. Pilchard tried to get Wendy's attention by rubbing up against her leg.

"Miaow!" cried Pilchard loudly and stuck out her paw.

"Er – I think she wants us to follow her," said Wendy.

"Let's go!" said Bob, and they set off after Pilchard.

Pilchard raced ahead, and led them to Scoop.

"Well done, Pilchard!" said Scoop with a big smile on his face.

"Can we fix it?" said Bob.

"Yes, we can!" shouted the others, as Lofty pulled the flags off Scoop.

"Thanks, everyone!" said Scoop. "And you know something," he said to Pilchard. "If they did let cats enter dog shows, you'd be the winner for sure."

Bob asked Mrs Percival, who was one of the judges, if it would be all right for a cat to enter a dog show.

"It's a most unusual request, Bob," said Mrs Percival. "But it may be possible. I'll see what I can do."

A little while later the show started. Farmer Pickles and Scruffty were the first to take part. Scruffty performed perfectly.

After all the dogs had been in the ring, Mrs Percival announced Scoop and Pilchard – the first ever cat to enter.

"Thanks, Mrs Percival," whispered Scoop. He gently tipped Pilchard onto the grass and gave her instructions.

The judges watched very carefully.

Pilchard walked forwards, sat down and even rolled over. And to everyone's amazement, including Scoop's, she finished off with a fancy back flip. The audience clapped and cheered.

"You have a very talented cat there, Bob," admired Farmer Pickles.

"And you have a very talented dog, too," replied Bob.

But Scruffty covered his eyes and wimpered. He knew he didn't have a chance of winning now.

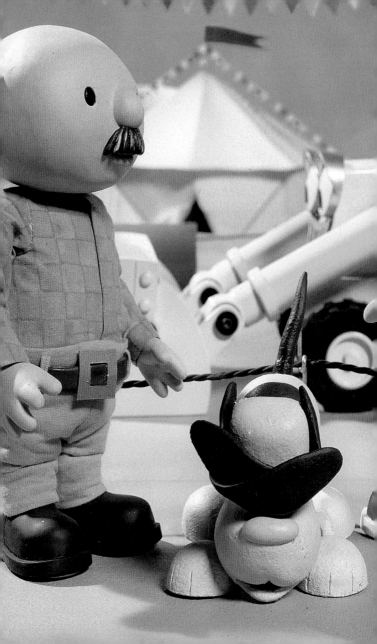

While the judges were making their decision, Bob and the team went to congratulate Pilchard and Scoop.

"That was brilliant, Pilchard!" said Scoop.

"Miaow!" purred Pilchard.

"If I hadn't seen it with my own eyes I would never have believed Pilchard could do all of those tricks," said Bob.

Everyone lined up for the prize-giving ceremony. There was silence as Mrs Percival carried over a trophy for the winner.

"I'm pleased to announce that the winners of this year's dog show are... Scoop and Pilchard! Well done!" said Mrs Percival.

Bob, Wendy and the machines all cheered, and Scruffty wagged his tail. Scoop felt very proud when Mrs Percival place the trophy in Pilchard's paws.

"Miaow!" cried Pilchard happily.

THE END!